W9-CTW-449   IED

JUNIOR DEPT

DATE DUE			
DEC 15 99			
JAN 02			
DEC 22 01			

Jackson MAY 4 1982
County
Library
System

HEADQUARTERS:

413 W. Main

Medford, Oregon   97501

The Christmas Tomten

by Viktor Rydberg · illustrated by Harald Wiberg

Freely adapted by Linda M. Jennings from a translation from the Swedish by Lone Thygesen Blecher and George Blecher.

Coward, McCann & Geoghegan, Inc.   New York

Library of Congress Cataloging in Publication Data Rydberg, Viktor, 1828–1895. The Christmas tomten. Translation of Lille Viggs äventyr på julafton. "Freely adapted by Linda M. Jennings from a translation by Lone Thygesen Blecher and George Blecher." Summary: On Christmas Eve, Vigg is invited to accompany the Christmas tomten on his rounds which include a stop at the Hall of the Mountain King. [1. Christmas stories. 2. Folklore—Sweden] I. Wiberg, Harald. II. Jennings, Linda M. III. Title. PZ8.1.R9Ch 1981 398.2'1'09485[E] 81–3225 ISBN 0–698–20528–6 AACR2

*I*t was Christmas Eve. In the middle of the snowy moor you could just see a thin wisp of gray smoke hanging in the frozen air. It came from the chimney of a little cottage, and in that cottage lived Mother Gertrude and her adopted son, Vigg. Mother Gertrude had been away since dawn, shopping for Christmas, in the town miles from their home.

Inside the cottage Vigg waited, his face pressed against the windowpane. The snow glowed pink in the sunset, but still Mother Gertrude had not returned. Darkness fell, and the stars shone out like beautiful flowers. Across the frosty wastes Vigg could hear something. It sounded like sleigh bells, but who could be coming to the cottage at this time? To Vigg's astonishment four tiny horses drew up outside, and the strangest little person jumped down from the sleigh. He had a curly white beard which reached to his feet, a long hat and shaggy-looking clothes. His little old face was covered in wrinkles, and his eyes shone kindly as he said to Vigg:

"Do you know who I am? I am the Christmas Tomten."

"I have heard of you," said Vigg. "Mother Gertrude says you are a nice old fellow."

"How would you like to come with me to deliver presents?" asked the Tomten.

Vigg looked out at the frosted snow and the star-spangled sky. "I would like it very much," he said, "but I must be back when Mother Gertrude returns."

"I will promise you that," said the Tomten.

Off they went, the little Christmas Tomten and the young boy, his cheeks rosy with excitement and cold. Vigg was only thinly dressed, but the Tomten wrapped a fur rug warmly around him. The four little horses flew across the snow, swift as the wind, and all the silver sleigh bells rang out happily in the still air. Soon they plunged deep into the forest. It was completely dark but for the occasional glow from a lonely cottage window. The trees were so tall that they seemed to reach the stars.

After a while the Tomten drew up by a small farm. "This is a good farm," said the Tomten. "The farmer works hard, and the animals are well-tended. The children, too, are delightful, though the boy is a bit high-spirited. We will certainly leave some presents here." And from a large chest under the seat of the sleigh the Tomten took out gifts to please the whole family: a clock for Father, a sewing box for Mother, a penknife for the boy, a book for the girl.

The room inside the cottage was lit by the light of a hundred candles decorating the Christmas Tree. What a peaceful scene! The family sat at the table while Father read them the story of the Nativity from a big, old Bible.

"I'm very fond of that baby he is reading about," remarked the Tomten. "But mind you, old Thor was a fine fellow, too."

"Who was old Thor?" asked Vigg.

"I'll tell you about him," said the Tomten. They both quietly left the room, with the gifts stacked just inside the door. "Thor was very tough on wicked folks," he went on. "He would hit them on the head with his big hammer. But people now believe the Christian way of peace is better than violence."

By now the Tomten and Vigg had reached a big barn. Inside they could hear a dull knocking sound. As they looked through the window they could see two little house trolls busily thresh-ing corn by the light of a lantern.

"Surely you can rest on Christmas Eve," said the Tomten.

"The harder we work the greater the pile of golden corn," replied one of the trolls.

"We'll all meet later in the Hall of the Mountain King," said the Tomten. "Don't forget." And leaving behind presents for the farmer and his family Vigg and the Tomten went on their way.

From cottage to cottage, from farm to farm Vigg and the Tomten went, delivering their gifts. Vigg knew some of the people well, like the old priest who had taught him his ABCs. His was a happy home, and the Tomten left some beautiful gifts there. As they traveled on through the deep forest they suddenly came across a very sad-looking house troll tramping along the road.

"Whatever is the matter?" asked the Tomten.

"I am running away," said the house troll, "for I cannot stand my present home any longer. Father drinks heavily, and Mother loses her temper. As for the children, they scream and cry from morning till night."

"Try to stay for just one more year," begged the Tomten. "If you go now, then any peace that is left will go with you. My presents may warm their hearts—and, who knows, by next year things could be better."

"Oh, very well," said the little house troll, and trudged back to the house, carrying some small parcels with him.

Clip-clop, clip-clop went the horses' hooves on the hard-packed snow. On, on through the forest they went, until, suddenly, ahead of them they saw gleaming through the trees a myriad of bright lights.

"What a large house," said Vigg as they drew nearer.

"Ah, here they are very rich," said the Tomten. "And they will receive many wonderful presents. Mind you, they are so grand that they probably will not think much of them."

Vigg's eyes were dazzled by the contents of the Tomten's chest. There were bracelets and buckles, rings and necklaces, there were stockings of the finest silk and rolls of rich satins and velvets. The Tomten pulled from the pile of glittering gifts a splendid golden star on a chain.

"Who is that for?" asked Vigg.

"Who else but the Master of the House," replied the Tomten.

In the big grand house the Tomten delivered all the presents. Even though they were so beautiful, what the Tomten had said was true. None of the richly dressed ladies and gentlemen showed any great excitement or pleasure. That was, except the Master of the House. When the Tomten told him that the golden star was a present from the King he danced for joy in front of the mirror.

"Just like a child," remarked Vigg.

"He is a child at heart," said the Tomten.

Finally the Tomten and Vigg arrived at the King's Palace. How splendid it was!

"I have some presents for the young Prince," said the Tomten, and once again he opened the chest. Vigg's eyes widened as he stared at all the wonderful things inside. There were thousands of model horses and soldiers, scores of toy ships and cannons, and, most remarkable of all, tiny people such as the King would have as his subjects—bricklayers and shoemakers, carpenters and weavers.

"The King's son must see the ordinary people as well as the soldiers and warships," explained the Tomten. "He must learn that when he is King he will be responsible for them all. And now," he went on, "off we go to the Hall of the Mountain King."

Vigg was silent as they traveled on. At last he said: "Everyone has had Christmas presents but me."

"I have not forgotten you," said the Tomten. And he pulled from the chest a plain pair of thick, hand-knitted woolen stockings.

"Oh!" said Vigg. "Is that all?"

"You need a new pair," said the Tomten.

"Mother Gertrude could have darned the old ones," said Vigg sulkily, thinking of the Prince's beautiful gifts.

The Tomten said nothing, but looked stern.

By now the two of them had reached a big high mountain and the Tomten halted the horses in front of a gap in the rock. "This leads to the Hall of the Mountain King," he said.

Vigg and the Tomten left the brightness of the snow to enter a terrifying blackness lit only by the glowing yellow eyes of vipers and toads. A particularly hideous-looking gigantic green toad was squatting nearby on a rock. Vigg pulled back, but the Tomten grasped his hand firmly and told him to be brave.

"Ugh," said Vigg, shuddering.

"You can only blame yourself for her appearance," said the Tomten. "When you envied the Prince his gifts she crawled out from under a rock, all swollen with dissatisfaction."

The two of them went deep into the heart of the mountain, until they reached a huge cavern, where hundreds and hundreds of little trolls stood, each one holding a flickering torch. In the center of the cave sat the King on his golden throne, and beside him was his daughter. She looked terribly unhappy, and her complexion was as pale as the silver dress she was wearing. "The Princess is ill," said the Tomten. "Unless she leaves the Hall soon and is able to breathe the fresh sweet air, she will die." He pointed to a gigantic set of scales, one bowl of which was laden with toads and vipers. "Those are the evil deeds of the world," he said. "For every good deed a golden weight is put in the other bowl to balance it. Only when the bowl containing the golden weights sinks to the ground can the Princess be free." Hardly had the Tomten spoken when he was called to make his report. When he spoke of the love and happiness that Christmas brought, the golden scale of goodness sank lower and lower to the ground. But then he came to Vigg, telling how ungrateful Vigg had been over the gift of the woolen stockings, and how envious of the Prince.

At this, one of the trolls put the huge green toad that Vigg had seen earlier into the scale of evil, and so heavy was the slimy creature that the scales started tilting the other way. Vigg hung his head as everyone in the Hall stared accusingly. But the Tomten had not finished. He was talking about Mother Gertrude now, of how she took in the orphan, Vigg, and loved him as her own son, and how she readily forgave him his mischievous ways. And now she had set off for the distant town in the snow and cold to bring Vigg all the little Christmas gifts she knew would please him.

As the Tomten finished speaking, the scales of goodness became weighted down with gold and came to rest on the floor of the cave. The Princess was free at last!

Vigg's eyes filled with tears as he thought of how very nearly he had condemned the Princess to eternal night. He was still crying when he woke up in his own little bed in the cottage on the frozen moor. The Tomten, the Mountain King, the Trolls, the Princess, all had vanished.

There, by the fireside, was Mother Gertrude. "I am home again, Vigg," she said. "See what I have brought you for Christmas." And she held out to him a pair of fine leather shoes such as he had always dreamed of owning. And to go with them Mother Gertrude had knitted him a pair of woolen stockings. Vigg stared at them in amazement, for surely they were the very same stockings he had seen in the Tomten's chest. He jumped out of bed and flung his arms around Mother Gertrude's neck. "Oh thank you," he cried. "You have brought me exactly what I have always wanted!"